A Robbie Reader

Money Matters: A Kid's Guide to Money

SAVINGS TIPS FOR KIDS

Tamra Orr

Mitchell Lane
PUBLISHERS

P.O. Box 196
Hockessin, Delaware 19707
Visit us on the web: www.mitchelllane.com
Comments? email us: mitchelllane@mitchelllane.com

MONEY MATTERS
A KID'S GUIDE TO MONEY

Budgeting Tips for Kids
Coins and Other Currency
A Kid's Guide to Earning Money
A Kid's Guide to Stock Market Investing
Savings Tips for Kids

ABOUT THE AUTHOR: Tamra Orr is the author of more than 100 books for children of all ages. She lives in the Pacific Northwest with her kids and husband and spends as much time reading as she possibly can. She has taught her own kids the savings tips you'll learn in this book, and she is doing her best to keep her savings accounts healthy and thriving as well.

PUBLISHER'S NOTE: The facts on which the story in this book is based have been thoroughly researched. Documentation of such research can be found on page 45. While every possible effort has been made to ensure accuracy, the publisher will not assume liability for damages caused by inaccuracies in the data, and makes no warranty on the accuracy of the information contained herein.

Library of Congress Cataloging-in-Publication Data

Orr, Tamra.
 Saving tips for kids / by Tamra Orr.
     p. cm.—(Money matters—a kid's guide to money)
 Includes bibliographical references and index.
 ISBN 978-1-58415-641-3 (library bound)
1. Saving and investment—Juvenile literature. I. Title.
 HC79.S3O77 2009
 332.0240083—dc22

                                              2008002260

Printing   2   3   4   5   6   7   8   9

PLB / PLB2

Contents

Chapter 1

SAVING UP FOR SPRING

Roberto looked out the window of the classroom. All he could see was gray, gray, and more gray. The sky was gray. The air was gray. The ground was gray. At one time the snow had been fresh and white, but that was days ago. Now it was muddy and melting. No wonder this time of year was Roberto's least favorite.

As if reading his thoughts, his teacher, Mrs. Bond, said, "What a dreary day it is!" Many of the other students nodded in agreement. It was the middle of winter, and the sun had been hiding forever. Spring seemed a long way away and summer almost impossible to imagine.

"I have an idea that might brighten up the day," their teacher continued. "I think you'll like it." Walking over to her desk, she picked up a stack of papers. "Take a look at these," she said, handing them out to the first person in each row.

Roberto read the chart on the handout. This *did* look interesting!

5TH-GRADE SAVINGS PROGRAM

POINTS AWARDED	FOR	PRIZES
5	every homework assignment turned in on time	10: coupon for ice cream at Hooper's Creamery
5	class participation	50: free book at Allan's Books and More
10	each A earned on quizzes or tests	100: pass to summer matinee movies at the mall theater
20	perfect attendance until the end of the unit	150: summer membership to the local YMCA

"Let me explain how this new idea works," said Mrs. Bond. "For the next few weeks, we are going to be studying about how important it is to save money. I thought saving up points might be a fun way to start. Every time you hand in a homework assignment on time, for example, you will get five points. You get another five points whenever you really participate in class—not just a single answer here and there, but join in to make comments, answer questions, and be involved. If you get an A on your quiz or test, you will get ten points. If you manage not to miss a single day for the rest of the unit, you will get twenty points! Does all of that make sense?"

Several students nodded. One hand went up.

"Yes, Tara?" asked Mrs. Bond.

"I like your idea, Mrs. Bond, but I'm not sure what we'll do with these points once we earn them," said Tara.

"If you look at the column on the right," Mrs. Bond answered, "you will see how you can spend your points. If you earn ten points, for example, you can get a free ice cream at Hooper's Creamery. Or you can skip the ice cream and try to save fifty points—then you can get a coupon for a free book from Allan's Books and More, over on Market Street. The next level of prizes is a free summer movie pass. The top award, for those with one hundred fifty points, is a summer membership to the YMCA. You can have a lot of fun there."

"You sure can," added Lyssa. "I went there last summer and they have a huge pool, plus they hold bike trips and teach you how to play tennis and other games. I had a blast!"

Luke's hand went up. "How do these things help us learn about saving?" he asked.

"The trick is to keep letting your points accumulate—even though you can take out your

Money Makers

Have you ever wondered how piggy banks got their name? It isn't because they look like pigs—that came later. The first banks were jars made out of *pygg*, a type of orange clay, so everyone called them piggy banks!

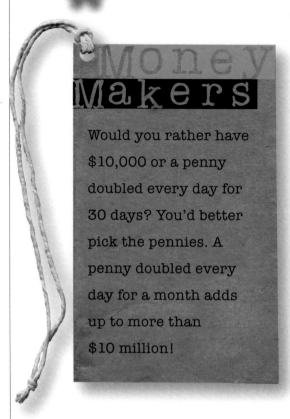

Money Makers

Would you rather have $10,000 or a penny doubled every day for 30 days? You'd better pick the pennies. A penny doubled every day for a month adds up to more than $10 million!

points at any time. One of the hardest things about saving money is that you have to wait to use it," replied Mrs. Bond. "It is often much easier—and more fun—to take it and spend it right away. You see something you want, you get it if at all possible. Yet if you save your money—or your points—you can wait and spend it more wisely. You can take the time to choose the right thing, or save up for something bigger and more important. You can even earn a little extra money through interest. Our savings program will show you how to 'save' points and then 'spend' them later."

Roberto looked back out the window at all the gray outside. He imagined what it would be like out there by the end of the school year. The snow would be gone and green grass would be there instead. The dark, bare tree branches would be filled with green leaves and the sounds of birds. With just a little imagination, he could almost feel a soft summer breeze blowing across the classroom.

"In this unit, we are going to learn about how banks work, how to open a savings account, how interest is figured, what credit is, and a lot more," added Mrs. Bond. "At the end, we

Bank **tellers** meet many people every day. They help customers put money into an account, take it out, switch it from one account to another, or answer your questions. In many banks, they work behind bulletproof glass to keep them safe.

will go on a field trip to a nearby bank and take a tour of what goes on behind the tellers' windows."

Several students began talking to each other. It was clear that everyone was looking forward to the next few weeks.

"Mrs. Bond, when does this savings program start?" asked Roberto.

"I plan to start on Monday. Why do you ask?"

Roberto chuckled. "I have a homework assignment due next week. I guess I know what I'll be doing this weekend!"

Mrs. Bond laughed, and so did a few other kids. Spring was still a long way away, but now it somehow seemed a little closer. It was time to start saving!

FROM SAVING TO SPENDING

2

Have you ever tried to save money for something? You might have saved your allowance or birthday money for an expensive item you wanted, or just for one of those "rainy days" your parents talk about. Maybe you have a jar in your room where you throw your coins left over from the day—maybe from lunch in the cafeteria or from playing games at the arcade.

Saving money is a good idea whether you are in elementary school, in college, or an adult. It is helpful to have funds when you want something or when an unexpected event occurs—like a flat tire on your bicycle or a last-minute invitation to a movie or party. It is nice not to have to rely on borrowing money from your parents and instead have some of your own put aside.

Money Makers

Experts recommend that adults always have two months' worth of bill money in their savings account just in case of an emergency.

Even though saving money is a terrific idea, it is not always very easy to do, no matter what age you are. If you have money in your pocket, it often seems much easier to spend it on an ice cream cone or a magazine after school than it does to put it away for something you won't be able to buy for months. Adults struggle with that too; they often have to save their money for future plans like vacations or retirement, as well as to keep money in accounts for unexpected emergencies such as a doctor's visit or a car, appliance, or home repair.

In other words, saving money takes determination and discipline for everybody. It means taking the time to look at the "big picture" of what you want. For example, let's say that three times a week, you spend money on the way home from school or just hanging out over the summer. Sometimes you buy an ice cream cone, while other times you buy a soda, a snack, or a magazine. Each time you spend about $2.50. If you add up that money, you might be shocked at how much it is.

Here is how much you spend in a week:

$2.50 x 3 = $7.50

Here is how much you spend in a month:

$7.50 x 4 = $30.00

Here is how much you spend in a year:

$30.00 x 12 = $360.00

$360!!

That is a lot of money. What else could you do with that much money? You could buy a cool video game system, an MP3 player, or a very nice new bike. You could even take some horseback riding lessons or buy new clothes.

Let's imagine that you get $5.00 a week as your allowance. You want to buy a new video game that costs $25. You know that you will have to save up your money for five weeks to get it. That sounds easy, but if you save every penny, you will not have anything left over for buying a soda, picking up a comic book, or getting an extra slice of pizza at lunchtime. Saving everything

Horseback riding is a rewarding but expensive hobby. If you're dreaming of someday taking lessons—or even owning a horse—put a poster up in your room to remind you of why you're saving.

and not keeping any is what is known as *unrealistic*. It's too hard to do and that makes it ever harder to continue doing it.

Here is another idea. You save $3 each week and keep $2 for those little things you want to get. How long will it take you to save for your game now? Even though you have to wait longer—a little more than eight weeks— it will be easier to save your money. You won't be tempted to take some from your savings stash.

To help keep your savings goals in mind, you might want to post photographs around your room of what you want. They would be a good reminder not to spend the money but to hold on to it for bigger things. You can make posters or hang pictures on your walls, on your mirrors, or on your school folders. Just put them where you can see them often. They will help you keep your eye on the big picture.

Out of Reach, Out of Mind

The number one key to saving money is to put it someplace where you cannot get to it easily. For example, you could put it in a special place in your room. Some people set up a series of envelopes that they keep in a desk drawer. Each envelope may have a different use. You could have one for spending NOW, and it would be used for books, snacks, or other small things. Another envelope might say LATER, and it would be for bigger things like a game or a bike. To keep your parents happy, you might add a third envelope that says FOR COLLEGE.

FOR COLLEGE

The problem with the envelopes is that for some people, they may be too close at hand, and therefore be too tempting to use. It takes a lot of willpower to stay out of them and not use up all the cash. It helps to put the money even farther away. Many people think that the best thing to do is to put it into a special account at the bank. There, it is out of reach—and even better, as you will soon find out, it can earn you some extra money while it is in there.

There are a lot of good questions to ask about banks. Which one is the best for you? How easy is it to open an account? How close is the bank to your house? Find out the answers before you make a choice.

Banking Those Bucks

Banks are definitely one of the safest places to put your money. It is protected there. It cannot be lost or misplaced. A government corporation known as the **Federal Deposit Insurance Corporation (FDIC)** guarantees that the money will be there, no matter what happens. No one else can get to it other than you (and perhaps your parents, since many banks will not allow **minors** to have accounts in their names only).

Before you head off to the nearest bank with your hard-earned money, however, you need to do a little research. Not all banks are the same. Different types of banks offer different services and charge different fees. Some of them have special programs just for young people. Don't pick a bank because your friend uses it or because it is closest to where you live. Instead, do some bank shopping and learn about how banks and savings accounts work.

Money Makers

Armored cars carry huge amounts of money from place to place. They are made out of Dyneema, a fiber that is 15 times stronger than steel! This makes them bulletproof and safe from all types of guns, as well as from grenades and even bombs!

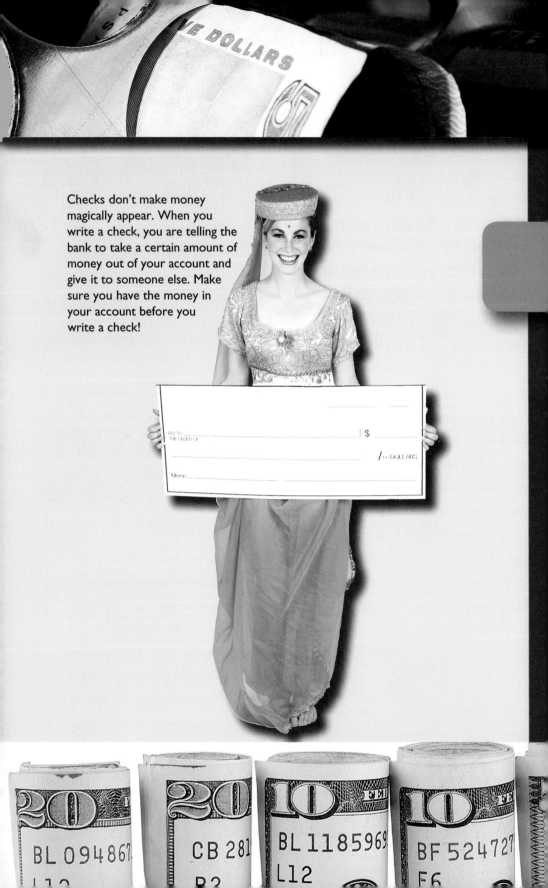

Checks don't make money magically appear. When you write a check, you are telling the bank to take a certain amount of money out of your account and give it to someone else. Make sure you have the money in your account before you write a check!

FROM CHECKING TO SAVINGS

Have you ever gone to the bank with one of your parents or a friend? There are often a lot of people in banks, filling out papers and standing in line. Most of them are there either to put money into the bank or to take it out. That is one of the main functions of any bank.

Banks are divided into **commercial banks**, **savings banks**, and **credit unions**. Commercial banks are the most common, and likely where you will go if you want to open a savings account. Individuals and businesses go there to **deposit** (put in) or **withdraw** (take out) money. A savings bank is very similar, but it deals mainly with savings accounts and making **loans**. Finally, a credit union is for people with some kind of common bond— usually they all work for the same company or have the same profession, such as the Teacher's Credit Union.

Meet the Staff

If you look around the bank, you will notice that people have different jobs in different places throughout the building. Most likely the people you see first are the **tellers**. These are the men and women who stand at the windows to take in and give out money. Each action they do for a customer is called a **transaction**. Along with handling money, tellers also answer questions about how much people have in their accounts, put coins in coin-counting machines, and cash checks.

Some of the people sitting at desks in the bank are the officers who help people open new checking and savings accounts. Others are in charge of taking loan **applications** (aa-plih-KAY-shuns) from customers who want to borrow money from the bank. People will take a loan to pay for improving their homes, going on vacation, buying a car, or starting other expensive projects. Other people around the bank might be the managers or even the bank's president.

If you look carefully, you might also see the bank's security officer keeping a careful eye out for anyone who looks suspicious.

Having a security officer in the bank helps to remind customers that their money is safe and also warns any possible criminals to stay away.

A photograph of the First National Bank in Edgeley, North Dakota, from the early twentieth century. How have the looks of banks changed since then? Why do you think they had bars everywhere?

For some people, robbing a bank can be a tempting idea, but almost no one ever gets away with it.

Ask Questions

When you go to a bank to talk about opening a savings account, have a list of questions with you. You should bring along a parent, too, because often banks require an adult to be present when talking about opening an account. A number of banks charge fees for their services. You should know what they are, or they might come as a real shock when you get your monthly **statement**. Often banks will offer special free accounts to young people to encourage them to open

accounts, so ask about that. In addition, you want to be able to get to your money when you need it.

Here are some good questions to start with:

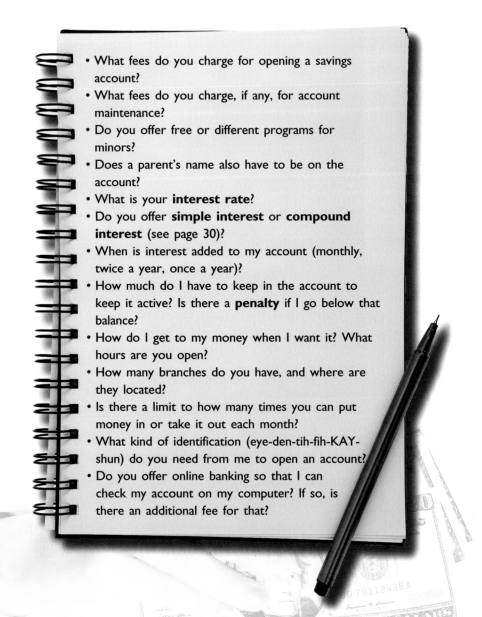

- What fees do you charge for opening a savings account?
- What fees do you charge, if any, for account maintenance?
- Do you offer free or different programs for minors?
- Does a parent's name also have to be on the account?
- What is your **interest rate**?
- Do you offer **simple interest** or **compound interest** (see page 30)?
- When is interest added to my account (monthly, twice a year, once a year)?
- How much do I have to keep in the account to keep it active? Is there a **penalty** if I go below that balance?
- How do I get to my money when I want it? What hours are you open?
- How many branches do you have, and where are they located?
- Is there a limit to how many times you can put money in or take it out each month?
- What kind of identification (eye-den-tih-fih-KAY-shun) do you need from me to open an account?
- Do you offer online banking so that I can check my account on my computer? If so, is there an additional fee for that?

The answers to all these questions are important. Write them down, then go to a few other banks and compare what you find out.

Make a Choice

Once you have found the bank that you like and that offers the most services for your money, you can open an account. You will be asked for identification (ID), which should include your birth certificate (ser-TIH-fih-kit), any picture ID you might have from school, and your social security card. Be sure to take those and a parent, since many times a parent's name will have to be on the account with yours. Once you arrive at the bank, here is the basic process:

1. Go to the New Accounts desk and say you would like to open a savings account.
2. The bank officer will give you a form to fill out. It will ask for basic information, such as your social security number, your address, and your contact information. Once you fill out the form, you'll need to sign it.
3. After everything is filled out and the bank officer has entered the information into the computer, you will give the bank officer the

New Accounts Here

money you want to deposit into the account. Sometimes there is a set amount you have to start with (usually $50 to $100), but some banks will accept less for a minor's account.

4. You will be shown how to fill out a deposit slip. It will look like this:

				DOLLARS	CENTS	
DEPOSIT TICKET	CASH					IF MORE THAN 5 CHECKS LIST ON BACK AND ENTER TOTAL HERE ↵
⊘PNCBANK	CHECKS PLEASE LIST SEPARATELY SHOWING	TRANSIT NUMBER				
FOR CREDIT TO THE ACCOUNT NAMED HEREON						
DATE _____	BANK'S TRANSIT NUMBER					
NAME _____						
ACCOUNT NUMBER REGIONAL ID	**TOTAL**					
	LESS CASH RECEIVED					
THIS DEPOSIT IS ACCEPTED SUBJECT TO VERIFICATION AND TO THE RULES AND REGULATIONS OF THIS BANK. DEPOSITS MAY NOT BE AVAILABLE FOR IMMEDIATE WITHDRAWAL.	**NET DEPOSIT $**					
☐ CHECKING ☐ SAVINGS ☐ CONSUMER ☐ BUSINESS						

FORM100635-0507

⑈6409⑈9910⑈

Since you just opened your account, the officer will write your account number on the slip. After this, you will use forms that have your name and number already printed on them. They are ordered at the bank and will come in the mail a week or so later.

Notice that the deposit slip has a place for how much money you are depositing (in cash amount and check amount). If you are depositing a check, you may want to deposit some of it and take the rest as cash. Whether you deposit all or part of a check, you'll need to sign the back of it. Be sure to date the deposit slip as well.

You can keep up to date on your bank accounts by going online. Your online account information is directly connected to the bank's records, so by the time you make a deposit and come back home, it will show up online.

How do you know how much is in your account? Most banks offer online banking, which means you can use your computer at home any time of the day to check your **balance**. Of course, the information is protected by a password, so

Even after you've opened a bank account, keep a special place at home to store money left over from each day. Once you've saved up a few bucks, you can add them to your savings account at the bank.

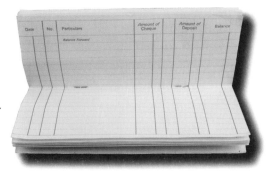

Although the bank keeps track of your credits and **debits**, you should keep track of them as well. Record them in a savings book (right) or check register. Compare your records with your bank statement to be sure no mistakes have been made.

only you and your parents can see it. You may also be mailed a monthly **statement** that shows your balance, your deposits, your withdrawals, and the interest you have earned.

Sometime in the future, you might also come into the bank and set up a checking account. It is not the same as a savings account. You still deposit money into it, but you remove money by either writing a check or using a **debit**

Unlike a savings account, a checking account lets you get to your money without going to the bank. One way to do that is by writing a check. First, fill out the day's date, who the check is for, how much you want to pay in both numbers and words, and then sign the check at the bottom.

card that is tied to your account. Have you seen your parents use one of those? Debit cards look a lot like **credit cards**, but there is one big difference: a credit card pays for things with someone else's money. You are borrowing it from somewhere else, and you will have to pay extra for the loan. A debit card takes the money directly out of your account, so it uses your money to pay for things. When you use your debit card, you are not paying extra for the items as you would be with a credit card.

There you go! You are ready to start saving your money in a bank. Now, let's take a look at how banks work—because that will explain how your money earns money, otherwise known as interest.

Money Makers

Some people do not keep their money in banks. When an empty house was fixed up in Johnstown, Pennsylvania, piles of old coins worth as much as $200,000 were found hidden in a hole in a wall. Some coins dated all the way back to 1793.

Roberto wanted to know more about how his money can make money. It was time to take a look at interest and how it works.

FROM INTEREST TO IRAs

Just what is so interesting about the word *interest?* You need to ask a lot of questions about it, but why? Is it really so important?

All businesses have to make money in order to stay open. After all, they have to pay for their electricity, heat, water, phones, and supplies in order to take care of their customers. They also have to pay their employees. One way banks earn money is through charging fees for opening and maintaining their customers' accounts. Is there another way? You bet! They do not just hold on to your money to be nice—it is their way of making a **profit**.

When you give your money to the bank, you might imagine that it sits somewhere hidden deep in a vault, just waiting for you to come and take some or add more. It may work that way in Harry Potter's Gringotts Bank, but not in real banks. Real banks turn around and lend your money to other people. In return, they charge that person interest, or a small percentage of the balance. For example, let's imagine your

bank has loaned someone $250,000 to buy a house. In return, they charge the person 6 percent interest. This is the bank's profit. Since they used your money to make the loan, they also pay you a part of that profit. This is the interest you earn on your money. If they give you 3 percent, then they still have 3 percent to keep. When you think about how many different loans they have out at a time, you can see how they make more than enough money to pay all their business costs.

When banks gave out low-interest loans in 2007, many people jumped at the chance to borrow money. However, when those interest rates went up, people could not pay back their loans. They **defaulted**—and lost their homes. The banks lost billions of dollars on these loans, and many banks had to close.

The Case for Compounding

There are two different ways that banks figure interest: simple and compound. Either way, the interest rates they offer are annual (yearly) rates, not monthly. With either method, the higher the interest rate the bank offers, the better!

Let's imagine that your bank gives you 3 percent simple interest. Your earnings will be based only on the amount you have deposited. To figure your monthly interest, the bank multiplies your balance by 0.03 divided by 12 months.

Compound interest, on the other hand, is calculated on your entire balance (deposits plus interest already applied). It is usually compounded daily, but applied monthly. Each day, the bank multiplies your balance by 0.03 divided by 365 days to see what your daily interest is, and then it adds that number to your balance. The next day, the bank figures the interest on the balance from the previous day. It adds the interest made every day during the month, and then applies it to your account at the end of the month.

If you haven't had the chance to save much money yet or it hasn't been in the bank for very long, it is hard to see much difference between what you can earn with simple and compound interest. However, if you are saving for the future, you will begin to see a big difference over the years. For example, let's see what happens to $500 over the course of 10 years.

SIMPLE VERSUS COMPOUND INTEREST*

YEAR	SIMPLE INTEREST	COMPOUND INTEREST
1	$515.00	$516.29
2	$530.00	$533.06
3	$545.00	$550.34
4	$560.00	$568.14
5	$575.00	$586.47
6	$590.00	$605.35
7	$605.00	$624.80
8	$620.00	$644.83
9	$635.00	$665.47
10	$650.00	$686.72

*at 3 percent interest

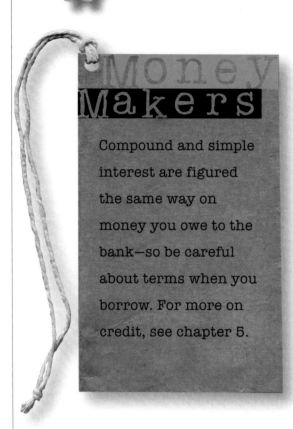

Money Makers

Compound and simple interest are figured the same way on money you owe to the bank—so be careful about terms when you borrow. For more on credit, see chapter 5.

With simple interest, it will take you 10 years to earn just a little more than what it took eight years to earn with compound interest. In a decade, simple interest earned you only $150, while compound interest gained you $186.72. Compound interest is the way to go!

Other Ways to Save

Are there bank accounts that help you save other than typical savings accounts? Yes, there are—although most of them are methods that are used mainly by adults who are **investing** their money in order to make more!

CDs, or Certificates of Deposit: A CD is something you buy for a set amount of money, which can be as low as $50. The bank holds on to your money for a certain amount of time, ranging from one month to five years. You are not allowed to withdraw your money until that time period is up. If you do, you have to pay a fee. If you keep it in there, your money will often earn a higher interest rate than if it were in a regular savings account.

IRAs, or Individual Retirement Accounts: IRAs are generally set up when you start working. You can use the money when you are old enough to retire. While it is in the IRA, the money

Some people make so much money, they can live off the interest alone. For example, say Miley Cyrus puts all her money into a savings account that gives her 3 percent simple interest. For every $1 million that she deposits, she will earn $30,000 each year.

can be invested in the **stock market**. Returns on IRAs can be quite high—but investments can also be lost if the stock market fails.

You work hard to save your money, so make the best choices you possibly can with it. Let the money you save earn you money for later. Ask questions, do your research, and make the wisest choices you can.

FROM CREDIT TO DEBIT

Have you ever borrowed money from your mom or dad against the allowance they were going to pay you at the end of the week or the birthday money Grandma was sending next month? Maybe you were invited to a movie with friends, or your favorite band just put out a new CD that you had to have right away. When you did this, your parents extended you **credit**—they gave you money that was not yet yours. It sounds wonderful—but borrowing always has a catch. For example, you'll be earning your allowance for the next week, but you won't see any extra spending money for two weeks.

Many banks offer their best customers some form of credit. They say, "Hey, you have been such a great customer for all these years that we want to offer you something extra. We are willing to lend you money to use however you want, and then we will give you lots of time to pay us back." Sounds like a great deal, doesn't it? But that credit comes with a high price tag.

Paying the Price

When people come to the bank to ask for credit or a loan, it is often for large and expensive items like a house or car, to start a business, or to pay off a large debt to someone else. Imagine if the bank agreed to loan you hundreds of thousands of dollars! It can be tempting to take it, but there is still that catch to keep in mind. When a bank loans you money, it charges interest on that money, and often that interest is rather high. Even though your payments back to the bank may seem small, most of the money is not paying down the balance; it is only paying the interest. You may borrow $50,000, but with all the interest adding up, you could end up paying thousands more than that.

The hardship can be even worse if your bank also gives you a credit card. Credit cards are reasonable to have if they are used appropriately. They are perfect in an emergency when money is needed—and you just don't have it. While all cards are issued by banks, some of them are made just for use in large stores such as Sears, JCPenney, or Nordstrom, or at certain gas stations. A credit card allows you to charge your purchases to the bank that issued it, and the bank pays the bill for you! Of course,

Money Makers

In 2008, the credit card debt in the U.S. was over $1.7 trillion. More than two million American homes had credit card debt of over $20,000, and the average consumer was walking around with four credit cards in his or her wallet.

in return, you get a statement that says you now owe that money to the bank—plus interest. Some interest rates are 20 percent or higher. At 20 percent, if you charged $100 and you paid the minimum payment of $9 per month, you would actually pay the bank $111. In addition, if you don't pay the minimum payment or you miss a payment, there is often another charge added to the balance. When you consider that these cards commonly also charge a membership or annual fee to use them, it is easy to see how a $100 purchase can quickly cost you $200. That is exactly what the credit card issuer hopes. Three-quarters of their profit comes from those **finance charges**, so they would rather you take your time in paying them back. If you pay your balance in full each month, however, most banks will not charge you interest.

Another option banks may offer is known as a **line of credit**. With this, the bank tells you that you can have a set amount of cash, but instead of giving it all to you at once, you can use it as you need it. That way if it turns out you don't need it all, you won't have to use it— or pay interest on it.

The Key to Credit

While credit is not offered to children, it is still important to understand. When you get dozens of invitations to sign up for credit cards, or when you go to the bank to talk about a college loan, this is all information that you will need to

Money Makers

Each year, teenagers in the United States earn over $140 billion from a combination of gifts and paychecks. No wonder they need savings accounts!

know so that you can ask the right questions, take the sensible offers, and ignore the unwise ones.

For example, it is helpful to realize that banks are not foolish enough to loan money to people they do not think will be able to pay them back. They will most likely do a **credit check** on credit card and loan customers. A credit check is an investigation into people's backgrounds. Have they had other loans? Did they pay on time? Do they have a lot of other debts? Banks want to see a strong credit (paying) history. All of these factors are important for the banks to know before they hand over the cash.

What happens if this is your first time taking a loan or line of credit? Some banks may require **collateral**. This is something of value that they can sell if you do not pay the money back like you are supposed to. Others may insist that you bring in a **cosigner**, a responsible person who is willing to say, "If this person doesn't pay back the loan, I will." That is a lot to ask of someone! Often it is going to be your mom or dad until you are old enough to get your own credit record established.

It is better to save than to borrow.

Credit Advice

If you do one day use a credit card—and most people do—then keep these things in mind:

- Always pay more than the minimum payment requested. In fact, you should always pay at least the minimum payment plus the monthly finance charge.
- If you can pay off the entire balance, do so.
- Use credit cards only for emergencies, not for regular bills or splurging.
- Keep track of your interest rates and be ready to pay off one and go with another one that has a lower rate. If you do transfer your balance, cut up your first card so that you still have only one.
- Always make your payments on time so that you do not get charged late fees.

It is always better to save first and then purchase something than to buy now on credit and pay the bank for months and months to come. Remember: The money that you pay toward your credit card every month is money you no longer have to buy other things you may want or need.

Money is an amazing thing. It is said that money "makes the world go round," and in many ways, it does. While spending can be fun, saving it and using it to get what you really want in life can be much more rewarding. It teaches you discipline, responsibility—and in the end, you still get to use your money for something you've always wanted. How is that for a deal?

There is no question that money is fun to have—and it can help you get the things you want. But remember, you have to use your money responsibly, and often the key to that is saving it instead of spending it.

TIME TO SPEND POINTS!

Roberto breathed deeply as he came into the classroom. Mrs. Bond had opened two of the windows, and a spring breeze was blowing in. The whole room smelled fresh and full of the promise of warm weather. After such a long gray winter, it was quite welcome.

"Good morning, Roberto," Mrs. Bond said. "Did you know that today is the first official day of spring?"

Roberto grinned. Apparently he wasn't the only one who was ready for winter to end.

The bell rang and Mrs. Bond took attendance. Everyone was there—they knew that today they would get their point totals, and no one wanted to miss it.

Luke wanted to spend his points on a movie pass for the summer. Many great new films were coming out, and he could not wait to see them.

"First of all, I want you to know how proud I am of all of you," she said. "Each one of you has done a great job. I know that it was hard for a few of you, but most of you kept your eyes on the goal and did wonderfully." With a flourish, she pushed the world map out of the way and on the board was everyone's points. Three students had earned and saved over 150 points; eight had saved more than 100—even after cashing in a few points for books and ice cream on the way.

"What did you learn about saving?" asked Mrs. Bond.

Tara raised her hand. "I had trouble deciding between the book and the YMCA membership," she said. "In the end, I'm glad I saved up for the membership."

"I kept watching the movie titles at the mall," said Luke. "I kept wanting to borrow from my allowance to see them instead of waiting for my points."

"I had a tough time earning those last five points, because getting my homework done with this nice weather has been really hard," Donny said. "But now I have exactly fifty, so I can get that book I wanted." He thought for a moment. "Maybe I shouldn't have cashed in those first ten points for ice cream."

"Those are the same kinds of temptations you will have when saving money," agreed Mrs. Bond.

"Hey, Roberto," said Tara when class was over. "Don't let me eat too much for lunch!"

"Why?" asked Roberto.

"Because even with the Y membership, I have ten points left over for free ice cream on the way home from school," she replied.

"Hey, I do too!" added Roberto. "An ice cream cone is the perfect way to celebrate the beginning of spring!"

BOOKS

Babour Publishing. *Money Doesn't Grow on Trees?! An Indispensable Guide to Money.* Uhrichsville, Ohio: Barbour Publishing, 2005.

Drobot, Eve. *Money, Money, Money: Where It Comes From, How to Save It, Spend It and Make It.* Toronto, Canada: Maple Tree Press, 2004.

Holyoke, Nancy. *A Smart Girl's Guide to Money: How to Make It, Save It, and Spend It.* Middleton, Wisconsin: American Girl, 2006.

Linecker, Adella C. *What Color Is Your Piggy Bank: Entrepreneurial Ideas for Self-Starting Kids.* Montreal, Quebec: Lobster Press, 2004.

Mayr, Diane. *The Everything Kids' Money Book: From Saving to Spending to Investing.* Avon, Massachusetts: Adams Media Corp, 2002.

Shelley, Susan. *Complete Idiot's Guide to Money for Teens.* New York: Alpha Books, 2001.

ON THE INTERNET

Dollars and Cents for Kids
http://www.banksite.com/kidscorner

Kids Bank.Com
http://www.kidsbank.com/index_2.asp

Moneyopolis: Where Money Sense Rules
http://www.moneyopolis.com/new/home.asp

BOOKS

Bochner, Arthur, and Rose Bochner. *The New Totally Awesome Money Book for Kids.* New York: New Market Press, 2007.

Harman, Hollis P. *Money Sense for Kids.* Hauppauge, New York: Barron's Educational Books, 2004.

Kay, Ellie. *How to Save Money Every Day.* Ada, Michigan: Revell, 2004.

Mack, Ryan O. *Easy-to-Understand Money-Saving Tips for Everyone.* Rockville, Maryland: Seaboard Press, 2006.

O'Neill, Barbara. *Saving on a Shoestring: How to Cut Expenses, Reduce Debt, and Stash More Cash.* New York: MJF Books, 2003.

ON THE INTERNET

Family Education's "Savings Accounts for Kids"
http://life.familyeducation.com/money-management/money-and-kids/48121.html?page=2

Hoffman Brinker and Roberts: "Credit Card Debt Statistics"
http://www.hoffmanbrinker.com/credit-card-debt-statistics.html

Kiplinger: Credit Card Payoff Calculator
http://partners.leadfusion.com/tools/kiplinger/card04/tool.fcs

Jokela, Becky Hagen. University of Minnesota Extension, "Helping Teach Children to Save Money," April 27, 2006.
http://www.extension.umn.edu/extensionnews/2005/teachchildrenmoney.html

Think Glink.com: "Personal Finance and Money Savvy Kids"
http://www.thinkglink.com/personal-finance.asp?subcategory=Money-Savvy-Kids

application (aa-plih-KAY-shun)—A form to be filled out and used to apply for something, such as a loan.

balance (BAL-ents)—The amount of money in an account, or the amount of money owed on a credit or loan account.

collateral (koh-LAA-tuh-rul)—Something of value that the bank can take from you if you can't repay a loan.

commercial bank (kuh-MER-shul bank)—The most common type of banking institution, offering checking and savings accounts for individuals and businesses.

compound (KOM-POWND) **interest**—Interest that is figured on the total balance in an account, including previous interest added.

cosigner (KOH-sy-ner)—A person who signs a credit contract stating he or she will pay the loan if the main borrower fails to do so.

credit (KREH-dit)—Money extended (loaned) to a person in return for payments with interest. Also, an amount added to an account.

credit card—A plastic card given out by banks and stores that allows consumers to charge their purchases to a bank; the consumer must repay the bank later, usually with interest and other added fees.

credit check—A look into the paying history of a consumer to make sure credit can be safely offered.

credit union—A type of banking institution for people with a common bond, such as a profession.

debit (DEH-bit)—Amount subtracted from an account.

debit card—A card that can be used like a credit card, but the funds come directly from an account in which the cardholder already has money.

defaulted (dee-FOL-ted)—Failed to repay a loan.

deposit (dee-PAH-zit)—To put something in, as putting money into a bank.

Federal Deposit Insurance Corporation, or **FDIC**—A government insurance company that guarantees that if a bank goes bankrupt or out of business, people who had accounts with that bank would not lose their money (up to $100,000 per person).

finance charges (FY-nants CHAR-jes)—Money a bank charges a customer for taking out a loan.

interest (IN-trest)—The money charged for a loan; also, money earned on the money kept in an account.

interest rate—The amount of interest charged or earned over time based on the balance.

investing (in-VES-ting)—Using money to make money.

line of credit—A set amount of cash a bank will let you borrow.

loan —Money given to someone that must be paid back.

minor (MY-nur)—A person who is under 18 years old.

penalty (PEH-nul-tee)—A fine.

profit (PRAH-fit)—Money earned after paying business costs.

savings bank—A type of banking institution that offers saving accounts and loans.

simple interest—Interest that is added to just the deposits made into an account, and not on the interest previously earned.

statement—A paper or online form that shows all transactions made on your accounts, including debits, credits, fees, and interest earned.

tellers—The staff in the bank responsible for dealing with customers' deposits and withdrawals.

transaction (tranz-AK-shun)—Any transfer of money (such as from customer to bank or bank to customer).

withdraw—To take something out, such as taking money out of a bank account.